Ladybird  Readers

Jon's Football Team

Series Editor: Sorrel Pitts
Text adapted by Coleen Degnan-Veness
Illustrated by Charlie Alder

LADYBIRD BOOKS

UK | USA | Canada | Ireland | Australia
India | New Zealand | South Africa

Ladybird Books is part of the Penguin Random House group of companies
whose addresses can be found at global.penguinrandomhouse.com.
www.penguin.co.uk   www.puffin.co.uk   www.ladybird.com

Penguin
Random House
UK

First published 2016
001

Copyright © Ladybird Books Ltd, 2016

The moral rights of the author and illustrator have been asserted.

Printed in China

A CIP catalogue record for this book is available from the British Library

ISBN: 978-0-241-25411-0

MIX
Paper from
responsible sources
FSC® C018179

Penguin Random House is committed to a
sustainable future for our business, our readers
and our planet. This book is made from Forest
Stewardship Council® certified paper.

Ladybird Readers

Jon's Football Team

Picture words

team

Ollie

Jon

football

goal

Jess

Ben Wills

Jon likes playing football.

Ollie and Jess like playing football, too.

Ollie and Jess play on Jon's team.

The moms and dads watch the team play.

Jon's team play football with the blue and yellow team.

The blue and yellow team get three goals! Jon's team do not get any goals.

11

The blue and yellow team
are very happy.

Jon's team are not
very happy.

Jon and his dad go to a big football game.

Jon's team go to the game, too.

Ben Wills gets four goals!

14

Jon and his team like
Ben Wills.

"Ben Wills is great!"
says Jess.

Jon's team play the blue and yellow team again.

Jess kicks the ball to Ollie.

"Very good, Jess!" says a man.

Ollie kicks the ball to Jon.

"Very good, Ollie!" says
the man.

Jon kicks the ball.

"Very good, Jon!" says
the man.

Jon gets a goal! The blue and yellow team do not get any goals.

Jon's team are very happy.

"Good game!" say the moms and dads.

The man speaks to Jon's team. He is Ben Wills!

"Good game, team," says Ben Wills. "Good goal, Jon!"

Jon is very happy!

Activities

The key below describes the skills practiced in each activity.

 Spelling and writing

 Reading

 Speaking

 Critical thinking

 Preparation for the Cambridge Young Learners Exams

1 **Look and read.**
Put a ☑ **or a** ☒ **in the box.** 📖 ✿

1 This is a football. ☑

2 This is Jon. ☐

3 This is Jess. ☐

4 This is Jon's friend, Ollie. ☐

5 This is Jon's team. ☐

2 **Circle the correct sentence.**

1 **a** Jon's team wear red and yellow clothes.
b Jon's team wear blue and white clothes.

2 **a** Jon is kicking the football.
b Jon's mom is kicking the football.

3 **a** The moms watch the teams play.
b The moms and dads watch the teams play.

4 **a** Jon's team do not get any goals.
b Jon's team are very happy.

3 Work with a friend. Look at the picture. Ask and answer *Who?* and *Where?* questions. 〇

Jon and his team like Ben Wills.

"Ben Wills is great!" says Jess.

Example:

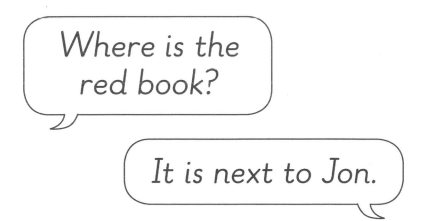

Where is the red book?

It is next to Jon.

4 **Circle the correct sentence.** 📖

"Good game, team," says Ben Wills. "Good goal, Jon!"

Jon is very happy!

1 **a** Ollie and Jess like playing football.

    b Ollie and Jess do not like playing football.

2 **a** Jon and his mom go to a football game.

    b Jon and his dad go to a football game.

3 **a** Ben Wills gets four goals.

    b Jon's dad gets four goals.

4 **a** Jon and his team like Ben Wills.

    b Ben Wills does not like football.

5 **Look at the picture and read the questions. Write one-word answers.**

Ollie kicks the ball to Jon.

"Very good, Ollie!" says the man.

Jon kicks the ball.

"Very good, Jon!" says the man.

1 Who kicks the ball to Jon?

_____Ollie_____ kicks the ball to Jon.

2 Who says, "Very good, Ollie!"?

The _____.

3 Who gets a goal?

_____

4 What is behind the goal?

A _____.

6 Ask and answer questions about Jon's team's clothes and hair with a friend.

Jon's team play football with the blue and yellow team.

The blue and yellow team get three goals! Jon's team do not get any goals.

10

Example:

Has Jon got brown hair?

No, he has not got brown hair.

7 **Read this. Choose a word from the box. Write the correct word next to numbers 1—5.**

Jon and his dad go to a big football game.

Jon's team go to the game, too.

Ben Wills gets four goals!

---

game   go   goals   great   like

Jon and his dad ¹ _____go_____ to

a football game. Jon's team go to the

² _____ , too. Ben Wills gets

four ³ _____ ! Jon and his team

⁴ _____ Ben Wills. "Ben Wills

is ⁵ _____ !" says Jess.

8 **Talk to your teacher about Ben Wills.** 🗨

1

> *Does Ben Wills like playing football?*

> *Yes, Ben Wills likes playing football.*

2 Is Ben Wills good at playing football?

3 Does Ben Wills like helping children play football?

4 Does Ben Wills talk to Jon?

5 Does Ben Wills like Jon's team?

9 **Match the two parts of the sentence.**

Jon's team play football with the blue and yellow team.

The blue and yellow team get three goals! Jon's team do not get any goals.

1 Jon's team play football with

2 Jon's team do not get

3 The blue and yellow team

4 Jon's team are not

5 The moms and dads

a are very happy.

b the blue and yellow team.

c any goals.

d watch the game.

e very happy.

10 Ask and answer *Can you?* and *Have you got?* questions with a friend.

Example:

Can you play football?

Yes, I can play football.

. . . a football?

. . . a favorite football team?

. . . kick a ball?

. . . football shoes?

11 **Write the questions.** 📖 ✏️

is　Where　he　?

1　Where is he?

this　your　Is　football　shoe　?

2　..

Are　your　these　shoes　?

3　..

kick　Can　it　I　?

4　..

Are　happy　they　now　?

5　..

12 Work with a friend. Look at the picture. Ask and answer questions about Ben Wills.

"Good game, team," says Ben Wills. "Good goal, Jon!"

Jon is very happy!

1 Where is Ben Wills?

He is behind Jon.

2 What is he wearing?

3 Where are his hands?

4 What is he saying?

13 **Circle the correct picture.**

1 Who does Jon play football with?

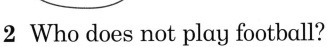

2 Who does not play football?

3 Who kicks the ball?

a  b

4 Where is the big football game?

a  b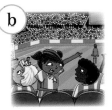

14 **Look and read.**
Write yes or no.

Jon and his team like
Ben Wills.

"Ben Wills is great!"
says Jess.

1 Jon is sitting on a chair. .... no ....

2 The blue bag is
in front of Jon. ....

3 Jess is in front of Jon. ....

4 A book is next to Ollie. ....

5 Ollie has got an
apple in his hand. ....

15 **Order the story. Write 1—5.** 📖

_____ Ben Wills gets four goals!

_____ Jon's team play football with the blue and yellow team.

_____ Jon, his dad, and his team go to a big football game.

__1__ Jon, Ollie, and Jess play football in the park.

_____ The blue and yellow team get three goals.

16 **Ask and answer the questions with a friend.** 💬 ❓

1

> ## What are Jon's team saying?

> ## We are very happy.

2 What are the dads saying?

3 What are the blue and yellow team saying?

4 Who is saying, "We are not great."?

17 **Talk to your teacher about football. Answer the questions.** ◐

1

What color is your football shirt?

It is red and white.

2 Have your mom and dad got a favorite football team?

3 Have you got pictures of football teams in your house?

4 Do your mom and dad watch football on TV?

5 Do you go to big football games?

18 Write the answer.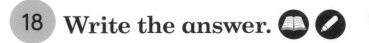

1 Has Jon got yellow socks?

No, he has not got
yellow socks.

2 Has Jon got a dad?

3 Has Jon got a cat?

19 **Find the words.**

football

goal

dog

team

mom   dad

book

Level 1

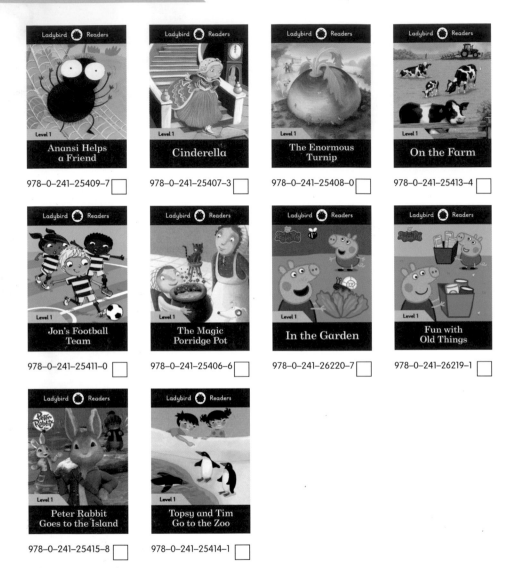

Anansi Helps a Friend 978–0–241–25409–7 ☐	**Cinderella** 978–0–241–25407–3 ☐

Ladybird Readers — Level 1
Anansi Helps a Friend
978–0–241–25409–7 ☐

Ladybird Readers — Level 1
Cinderella
978–0–241–25407–3 ☐

Ladybird Readers — Level 1
The Enormous Turnip
978–0–241–25408–0 ☐

Ladybird Readers — Level 1
On the Farm
978–0–241–25413–4 ☐

Ladybird Readers — Level 1
Jon's Football Team
978–0–241–25411–0 ☐

Ladybird Readers — Level 1
The Magic Porridge Pot
978–0–241–25406–6 ☐

Ladybird Readers — Level 1
In the Garden
978–0–241–26220–7 ☐

Ladybird Readers — Level 1
Fun with Old Things
978–0–241–26219–1 ☐

Ladybird Readers — Level 1
Peter Rabbit Goes to the Island
978–0–241–25415–8 ☐

Ladybird Readers — Level 1
Topsy and Tim Go to the Zoo
978–0–241–25414–1 ☐

Now you're ready for Level 2!

Notes
CEFR levels are based on guidelines set out in the Council of Europe's European Framework. Cambridge Young Learners English (YLE) Exams give a reliable indication of a child's progression in learning English.